Bordaria
Difendere con Coraggio

Scholastic Canada Ltd.
604 King Street West, Toronto, Ontario M5V 1E1, Canada

Scholastic Inc.
557 Broadway, New York, NY 10012, USA

Scholastic Australia Pty Limited
PO Box 579, Gosford, NSW 2250, Australia

Scholastic New Zealand Limited
Private Bag 94407, Botany, Manukau 2163, New Zealand

Scholastic Children's Books
Euston House, 24 Eversholt Street, London NW1 1DB, UK

POP & F!ZZ

Text, design and illustration copyright © Lemonfizz Media, 2010.
Cover illustration by Britt Martin.
Internal illustrations by Lionel Portier, Melanie Matthews and James Hart.
First published by Pop & Fizz and Scholastic Australia in 2010.
Pop & Fizz is a partnership between Paddlepop Press and Lemonfizz Media.
www.paddlepoppress.com
This edition published under licence from Scholastic Australia Pty Limited
on behalf of Lemonfizz Media.

First published by Scholastic Australia in 2010.
This edition published by Scholastic Canada Ltd., 2011.

Library and Archives Canada Cataloguing in Publication

Park, Mac

Tornados / Mac Park ; illustrations by Melanie Matthews, Lionel Portier and James Hart.

(Boy vs beast. Battle of the worlds)

ISBN 978-1-4431-0750-1

I. Matthews, Melanie, 1986- II. Portier, Lionel

III. Hart, James, 1981- IV. Title. V. Series: Park, Mac. Boy

vs beast. Battle of the worlds.

PZ7.P2213To 2011   j823'.92   C2010-907357-6

6 5 4 3 2 1   Printed in Canada 116   11 12 13 14 15

BATTLE OF THE WORLDS

TORNADOS

Mac Park

POP & F!ZZ

SCHOLASTIC

Prologue

Once, mega-beast and man shared one world. But it did not last. The beasts wanted to rule the world. They started battles against man. After many bad battles between beast and man, the world was split in two. Man was given Earth. Mega-beasts were given Beastium.

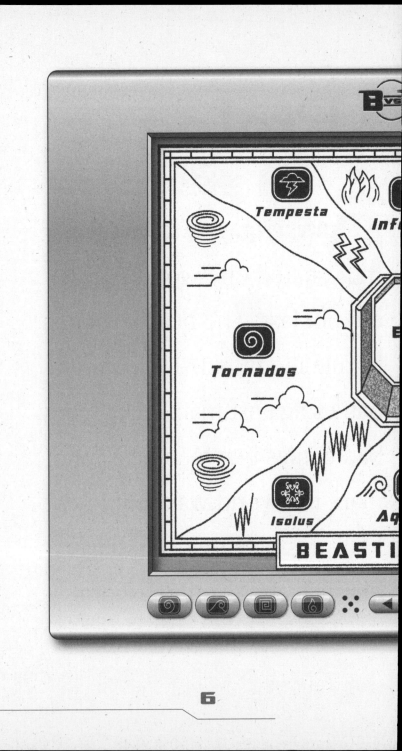

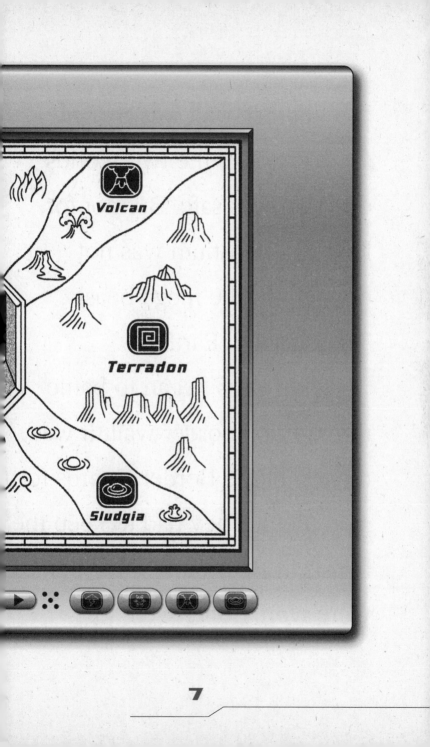

Volcan

Terradon

Sludgia

A border-wall was created. It closed the two worlds off. Man was safe. But not for long . . . Beastium was not enough for the mega-beasts. They wanted Earth.

The beasts began to battle through the border-wall. It was the job of the Border Guards to stop them. They had to keep the beasts in Beastium. Some battles were won. Some were lost.

Battles won by the beasts gave them more power. The beasts earned new battle attacks. Battles won by the Border Guards earned them upgrades. Their battle gear could do more.

Five boys now guard the border-wall. They are the Bordaria Border Guards. They are in training to become Border Masters like their dads.

The Bordaria Master Command

The Border Guards' dads and granddads are the Bordaria Master Command. The BMC helps the Border Guards during battle.

The Border Guards must learn. The safety of Earth depends on them.

The BMC rewards good Border Guard battling. Upgrades can be earned for sending beasts back into their lands. New battle gear can also be given to Border Guards who battle well.

If they do not battle well, the Border Guards will lose upgrades and points. Then they will not be given new and better gear.

Kai Masters is a Border Guard in training. His work is top secret. He must protect Earth. The BMC watches Kai closely. Kai must not fail.

Let the battles commence!

Chapter 1

Kai Masters was having lunch. He was at Burgers are Best. He loved their burgers. The radio was on. Kai was just about to eat his burger when a news flash came on.

"Very bad winds and dust storms are coming!" the voice said.

"Anyone outside should go home. Stay off the roads. Please stay in your homes. Wait there until it's safe."

That's odd, thought Kai. *We don't get wild wind storms here. Is this the work of beasts again?*

Kai Masters was a Border Guard. He guarded the wall between Earth and Beastium. And kept beasts in their lands.

He and his dogbot, BC3, battled beasts. Beasts that wanted to take over Earth.

Kai was a good Border Guard. But he was still learning. One day, Kai hoped to be a Border Master. Kai's dad was a Border Master. And so was his granddad.

Kai's dad was part of the Bordaria Master Command now. The BMC. The BMC helped Kai in battles.

Kai left his burger on the table. There was no time to eat it. He ran out of Burgers are Best. BC3 was waiting for him outside. The dog was a gift from the BMC. It was built for battle. BC helped Kai do his job.

He was Kai's buddy, too.
Kai called him BC for short.

BC had his fake fur on.
Kai put it on him when they
went out.

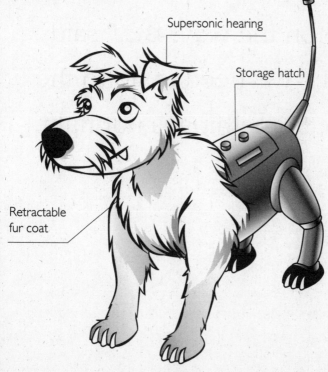

Supersonic hearing

Storage hatch

Retractable
fur coat

It made BC look like a real dog. BC hated it! It was itchy. He couldn't wait for Kai to take it off.

"Very bad wind storms are on the way, BC," said Kai. "We need to go to the lab! Something is not right."

Chapter 2

Kai and BC lived in a lighthouse. It had been in Kai's family for years and years. It looked really old from the outside. The inside was totally new. It had been set up for a Border Guard.

When Kai got home, he took BC's fur off.

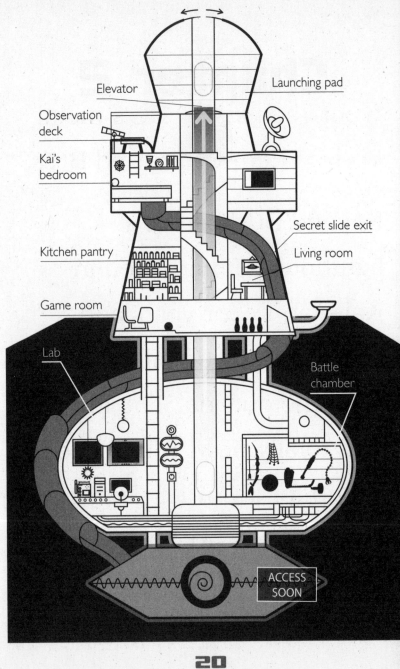

Elevator

Launching pad

Observation deck

Kai's bedroom

Secret slide exit

Living room

Kitchen pantry

Game room

Lab

Battle chamber

ACCESS SOON

Kai hit a button. The fur went back inside BC's metal body. Then Kai pushed BC's talk button.

The dog began to talk. "Dust is bad," said BC. "Can't see much." BC's tail was wagging. That always meant there was trouble.

Kai could hear the wind outside.

WOOOOOO WOOOOOSH

"The wind is blowing round in circles," he said. "Like little tornadoes!"

"We need to get a sample of it," said BC. "Maybe a beast from Beastium is coming."

"Maybe," said Kai. "A beast could be trying to come through the wall again."

Chapter 3

Kai went into his bedroom.
He went up the ladder.
Then he climbed out onto
the deck. The deck had a
glass roof. And two glass
walls. One wall was made of
brick.

On the brick wall was a
big photo of the beach.

Kai pushed a button on the wall. The photo slid down. A big touch screen was hiding behind the photo.

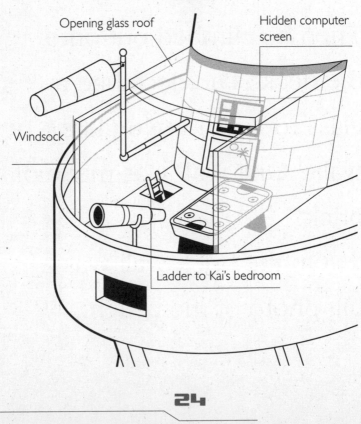

DECK

Opening glass roof

Hidden computer screen

Windsock

Ladder to Kai's bedroom

Kai touched "roof open" on the screen.

The glass roof slid open. Next he touched "windsock." The windsock came out from the wall. It went up into the air. It filled with wind. Then the windsock closed.

Then it came back inside.

Kai touched "roof close."
He took the windsock.
Then he went to the kitchen.
BC was waiting for him in
the pantry. "Can I push the
secret button?" asked BC.

"Go for it," said Kai as he
looked for something to eat.
*No snacks for me to eat here.
I'm so hungry*, he thought.
*I wish I'd had time to eat my
burger.*

BC pushed the button with his nose. It was under the pantry shelf.

The pantry's back wall started to move. It slid open. Kai and BC went in behind the wall. They went down the ladder into the lab. It was under the kitchen.

The lab was filled with top-secret tools. Tools for learning all about beasts.

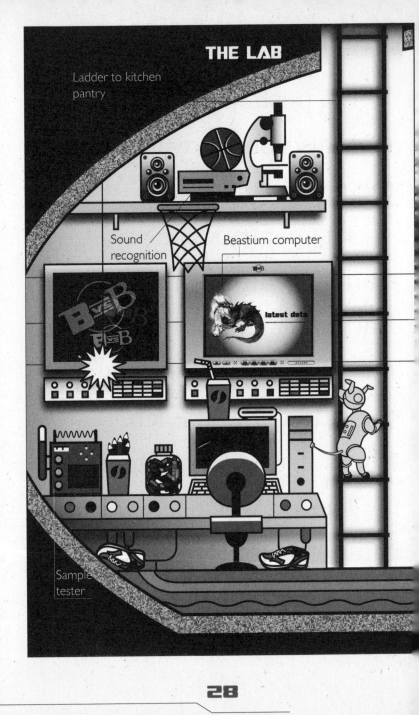

THE LAB

Ladder to kitchen pantry

Sound recognition

Beastium computer

latest data

Sample tester

Kai put the windsock
into the sample tester. He hit
the test button on his
computer.

"Rock and air lands," said
Kai. "Yes. Dirt and wind."

"We battle rock beasts again?" asked BC.

"No," said Kai. "I think it's the air land. The wind goes in circles. Just like in the air land, Tornados."

Kai hit the air land button. *I hope I'm right,* he thought. Then the computer flashed again. A card popped up on the screen.

"This beast looks mean,"

BEAST I.D.

TORMEGADACTYL
Mega peck and flap power

Strength	★★★★★
Attack Power	★★★★★
Speed	★★★★★

said Kai. "Let's go get our battle gear. This will be a hard battle."

Chapter 4

There was another secret room behind the lab. It was the battle chamber. It had all the battle gear. Kai took out his Border Guard Card.

Kai pushed the card into the computer. Then he took it out again. The computer flashed.

Name........... **Kai Masters**
Rank............ **Border Guard**
Guard Post...**Lighthouse**
Age..............**12**
Home Element... **Fire**

41352461

Bordaria
Difendere con Coraggio

Then there was a loud

noise.

CLUNK! BANG!

Whiiiiir!

BANG!

The bricks in the wall behind them began to move. Four bricks moved to make a hole. Kai and BC went through the hole into the room.

The room had three walls. The walls were filled with battle gear. The last wall had a screen over it.

Kai couldn't get to that wall. "I'm so over that!" said

Kai. "When will the BMC let me have things from the other walls?"

Kai saw something on the second wall. "I bet we still can't have things from this wall," he said.

"I want this," said Kai. He went to the middle wall. Kai tried to take a jet pack. He waited for the locked sound he always heard.

But the jet pack came off
the wall. "Yes!" said Kai.
"At last we can have things
from the middle wall!
Look at this, BC!"

ASTRO JET STRIKER

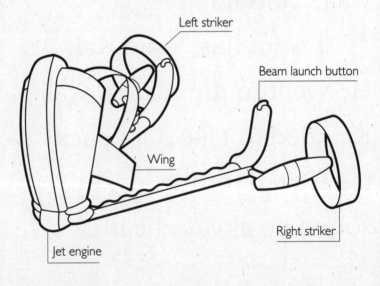

Left striker

Beam launch button

Wing

Jet engine

Right striker

"This can help me fly in strong winds. And it can make its own strong winds," said Kai.

"Good for air battles," said BC.

"We can pick one more thing from the battle chamber. What about that thing on the middle wall?" said Kai.

Kai read the tag. "It shoots rocks," he said. "That could be useful." Kai went to take it. He heard a noise.

CLUNK! GRRRR CLUNK!

Then a computer voice said,

"No more from here."

"Oh well," said Kai. "We got to have one thing from the middle wall."

Kai went back to the first wall.

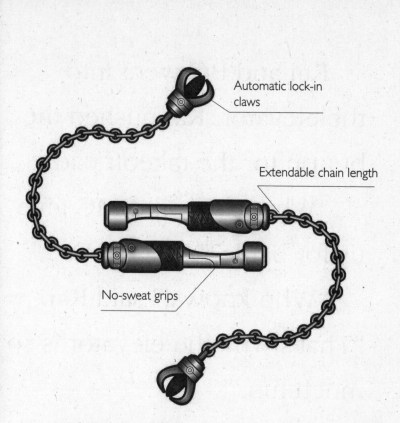

Automatic lock-in claws

Extendable chain length

No-sweat grips

"This looks good," Kai said. "These chains could be very handy." He took the chains. "Time to go then, BC."

Kai and BC went into the elevator. Kai pushed the button for the takeoff pad.

"What else will BMC give us for battle?" asked BC.

"Who knows," said Kai. "That's why the elevator is so much fun."

The elevator went to the top. Its door opened. Kai and BC were on the takeoff pad. They were ready for battle.

"The BMC gave you a jet pack, BC," said Kai. "And mine now has power boosters. That will be handy." Just then Kai's orbix beeped.

The orb was a small computer. It had lots of good stuff on it. And it could be used in battle. The BMC also used it to talk with their guards.

"You got another upgrade, BC," said Kai.

BC upgrade
Eye lasers

Kai hit the light button on the orb. The lighthouse roof opened. The takeoff pad lit up with light. The light went into the sky.

It took Kai and BC with it.

Chapter 5

Kai and BC landed on top of white clouds. It was very bumpy. They bounced about like balls.

"This is Tornados," said Kai. "The wind is strong. We have to get down through the clouds."

Kai and BC set their jet packs to high. They tried to push down, but they were thrown back up. They were back where they started.

Kai and BC bounced around. "How can we get past the clouds?" asked BC.

"Let's try my power boosters," said Kai.

Kai held BC. He hit the booster button. He and BC shot through the clouds. "That was so easy," said Kai. "These power boosters are great."

Kai let go of BC. "Let's look around." He and BC moved slowly in the air. It was quiet and still. Then BC's tail began to wag. "What is it, BC?" asked Kai.

"Something is coming," said BC.

Kai turned to look. But it was too late. Birds were flying straight for him. They dived at Kai.

There were lots of them. They pecked him with their sharp beaks.

 Kai was
being pecked
and pecked.
And he was
rolling away.
"Help, BC," he

said. "Use your eye lasers."

BC hit the birds with his
lasers. One by one they fell
away.

"Thanks, BC," said Kai.
"Those birds hurt."

"Eye lasers are good!" said BC. And then his tail wagged once more. That was not good.

Kai looked around the air land. He saw something this time. "It's another one of those birds," said Kai. "Do your stuff, BC."

BC hit it with his lasers. But the lasers did nothing. The bird just kept coming.

"Oh, no," said Kai. "It's not the same kind of bird. I'm not sure what it is. It's smaller than the one we saw in the lab. And more are coming."

The birds began to flap their wings. They made a wind that pulled Kai and BC into them.

"They are sucking us in," said Kai. "And they aren't birds. They are some kind of baby beast."

Kai grabbed hold of
BC. Then he hit the power
booster button on his jet
pack.

But it was too late.
The beasts flapped
their wings again.
This time the wind
pushed Kai and BC far back.
They were thrown a long
way.

The place they landed in was very stormy. Kai and BC raced back to the air land. This time they were ready.

Kai threw his beast chains. They grew longer and longer. Long chains went round and round one baby beast. Kai got it easily. "Use your lasers," said Kai. BC took a shot.

"Got it," said BC. Kai took the chains off the beast. It fell away. The chains went back down to their small size.

"Two more coming," said BC. Kai threw the chains.

WOOOP

WOOOP

Even longer chains came out. They went round and round another beast. Again BC hit it with his lasers.

The beast fell back deep into the air land.

"One more to go, BC," said Kai. "Watch out. It's coming for you."

Kai quickly threw the chains. He got the beast just before it got BC. "That was close," said Kai. "We've sent them back where they came from. Come on, let's keep going."

Chapter 6

Kai and BC pushed through the wind. It was a hard ride. Wind blew around in circles. Then a huge wind blasted them. It sent them tumbling over and over.

woosh whhiiiir woosh

It was going round and round really fast. It was turning into a big twister.

"Get behind me quick, BC," said Kai. He turned on his air-strikers. They were set to top-speed. The two air-strikers made their own winds.

The winds were strong. They went around in circles. Kai had made his own twisters.

Kai's twisters pushed the big twister back. "Hang in there, BC," said Kai. "We're beating it."

But then there was a loud noise.

THWACK THWACK

A huge beast was inside the big twister. Kai saw two big blue wings slap together. The wind from the wings sent Kai and BC rolling. Kai took out his orb. He took a photo. *I hope the BMC finds this one for me fast,* he thought. A card popped up onto the orb's screen.

BEAST I.D.

TORMAXIDACTYL
Beware this beast's toxic breath

Strength	★★★☆☆
Attack Power	★★★★☆
Speed	★★★★★

Kai looked up at the beast. It was getting ready to flap again.

THWACK

threw the chains. They went round the beast.
the beast was strong. It pulled Kai in.

Aaaargh what's coming out of its mouth?

It's green gas!

e beast's breath was toxic.
i was asleep. He could not
ht.

The gas wore off. Kai slowly woke up. He gripped the Astro-Striker.

I'll get the beast.

The beast has bad breath! Too much and you might never wake up.

Let's stop it before it gets us.

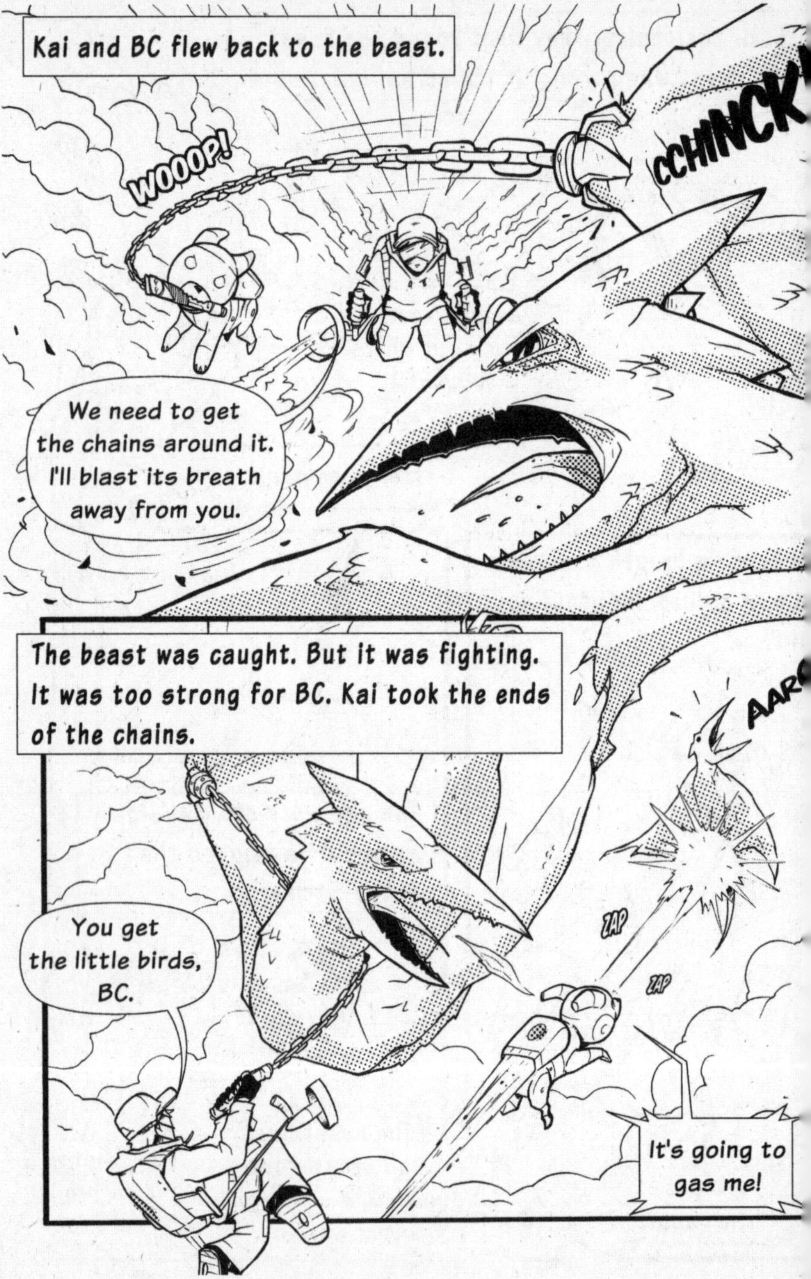

Kai and BC flew back to the beast.
WOOOP!
CCHINCK!
We need to get the chains around it. I'll blast its breath away from you.
The beast was caught. But it was fighting. It was too strong for BC. Kai took the ends of the chains.
You get the little birds, BC.
ZAP
ZAP
It's going to gas me!

Chapter 7

Kai was on the border wall.

He held BC in his arms.

The dog was not moving.

BC had been hit with too

much gas. Even for a dogbot.

BC could not wake up.

What can I do? thought Kai.

Just then Kai's orb

beeped.

Kai looked at the beast.

It was getting closer.

There wasn't much time.

He did BC's jetpack up.

Then he opened the orb.

There was a bottle sitting inside the orb. It was filled with gold oil. Kai took it out. *It's from the BMC,* he thought.

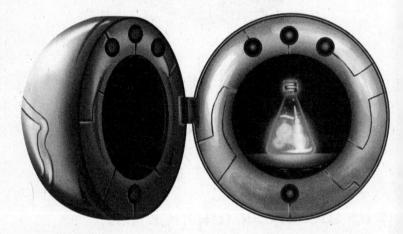

I'll put some oil in BC's ears, thought Kai. He opened the bottle. Kai tipped the gold oil into BC's ear. It went in. And it began to work.

The dogbot started to move. "Yes!" said Kai. You're waking up. Are you okay, BC? Do you think you can battle?"

"You bet," said BC.

"We only have one chain," said Kai.

"I can take one end," said
BC. "I'll go behind. You go
in front."

"Good plan. Let's wrap
this beast up once and for
all," said Kai.

"It must not crash through
the wall. We must stop it."

Kai and BC flew at the
beast.

BC flew behind it.

He took one end of the

chain with him.

The beast didn't even see him. It was looking at the wall.

Kai flew to the front of the beast. He took the other end of the chain with him.

Kai and BC went around the beast. Once, twice, three times. The beast was trapped.

It made a huge noise.

Then Kai took the chain
around the beast's mouth.
"No more bad breath for us,"
he said.

Chapter 8

Kai looked at the beast.
It was trapped.

The beast could not
move. "Time to send this
beast back to where it came
from, BC," said Kai.

He took both ends of the
chain. He locked
them together.

Kai used his power boosters on top speed. And he turned his air strikers on. A huge wind came from the strikers. The wind sent the beast back deep into the air land.

Kai took out his orb. He used it to bring the beast chains back to him.

"Beast gone for good?" asked BC.

"I think so," said Kai.

Then Kai heard his orb beep. "It's a message from the BMC," said Kai.

"But I don't know what it means," said Kai.

"What does the BMC say?" asked BC.

"Borderland beast," said Kai. "Is that two beasts in one? A beast from two worlds? But that could never happen. Time to go, BC. I'm so hungry!'

Kai keyed in:

Bright light shone on Kai and BC. Then it went back up into the sky. It took Kai and BC with it.

Earth was safe once more. Or was it?

TORMAXIDACTYL

This beast has had the wind knocked out of it

Battle Plays ★ ★ ★ ★ ★

New Attacks ★ ★ ★ ★ ★

Energy ★ ★ ★ ★ ★

BORDER GUARD BATTLE STATS

Kai Masters

Had a blast in this battle

Battle Plays ★★★★★

Upgrades ★★★★★

Bonus Items ★★★★★